Stories of
Merlin

Retold by Russell Punter

Illustrated by Gustavo Mazali

Reading consultant: Alison Kelly
University of Roehampton

Contents

Chapter 1

Birth of a legend

Long, long ago, so legend says,
a beautiful Welsh princess had
a son. She named him Merlin.

Merlin's father was a mystery.
Some tales said he was an angel.
Others told of a wicked demon.

Whoever he was, he gave his
son amazing, magical powers.

As a boy, Merlin was careful to hide these powers. He didn't want people to be afraid of him.

But it wasn't long before the mighty kings of Ancient Britain put his magic to use...

Chapter 2

The dragon tower

King Vortigern watched in
horror as the walls of his new
castle crashed down.

"What's going on?" he roared at his head builder. "That's the third time this has happened."

"I don't understand it, sire," trembled the servant. "The walls just won't stay up."

7

"How can I protect myself from Ambrosius's men without a castle?" sighed Vortigern.

Ambrosius was the true king. Vortigern had stolen his crown, and Ambrosius's followers wanted revenge.

Vortigern knew he had to do something before they attacked. "I must speak to my wise men."

"You need more than mortar to hold the bricks together," croaked one of his advisers.

"You must mix it with the blood of a boy whose father wasn't human," added another.

It sounded an impossible task. But Vortigern sent his men to find such a boy.

After weeks of searching,
Vortigern's men finally returned.
"We have him, your Majesty."

"What's your name?"
Vortigern asked the small boy.
"Merlin," he replied.

11

"Do you know why you're here, Merlin?" asked Vortigern, drawing his sword.

"Yes, your Majesty," Merlin said, calmly. "But my blood won't help your castle stay up."

12

"But my advisers..." began
Vortigern.

"...are fools," finished Merlin.
"I'll show you what's wrong."

He waved a hand. The
earth below one tower
magically faded away to show
what was underneath.

"There!" said Merlin. For a second, the king saw a vast expanse of water.

I can't believe my eyes!

Vortigern ordered his men to dig under the tower until they reached the water.

"Now all we have to do is drain the pool," said the king.

"I'm afraid that's only half the problem," Merlin told him.

At that moment, two massive dragons burst out of the pool.

Vortigern and his men looked on, horrified, as the ferocious beasts fought.

At first, the white dragon was the stronger.

16

Then its red opponent gave
a blood-curdling cry. It flew at
the white dragon, fangs bared.

It tore into its enemy's throat.
The white dragon thrashed
around. Then it lay still.

17

With a flap of its wings, the red dragon flew up and out of the tower.

"Your castle will be safe now," declared Merlin.

Vortigern sighed with relief.

"But you will not," Merlin warned. "Soon the true king will take your place." With that, he vanished.

Vortigern was the first king to call on Merlin's mystical powers. But he wouldn't be the last.

Chapter 3

The sword in the stone

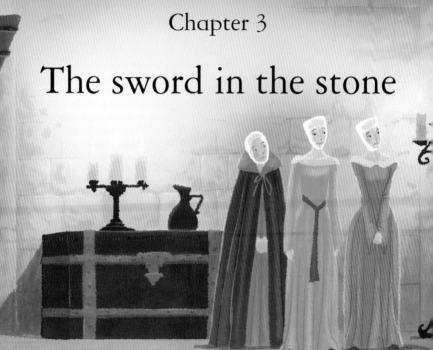

Sure enough, Ambrosius got
the crown back. When he died,
many years later, Merlin helped
his brother, Uther, become king.

One day, Uther asked Merlin to look after his newborn son, Prince Arthur. Merlin agreed, but he was worried.

"These are dangerous times, sire," he said to Uther. "Let me hide the prince until he's ready to be king."

21

Uther didn't want his son taken away. But he knew Merlin was always right.

So, one dark night, Merlin smuggled the baby prince out of the castle and into the forest.

Merlin took Arthur to a
knight named Sir Ector.

"Guard him with your life,"
Merlin ordered.

"I will treat the boy as if he
were my own son," replied Ector.

The knight was as good as his word. He brought up Arthur to be a brave, kind young man.

Arthur enjoyed his life in the forest. He and Ector's son, Kay, became best friends.

24

Every so often, Merlin visited Arthur and taught him about dragons, mystery and magic.

Arthur never knew he was a royal prince. Then, suddenly one winter, King Uther died.

Merlin acted quickly. He sent messages to the most powerful men in the land.

"Come to London at once," he told them. "The new king will be revealed to you there."

When the noblemen arrived, Merlin led them to a nearby square. There stood a stone.

Buried deep in the stone was a magnificent sword. Merlin read out some words carved on the stone.

"Whoever pulls out the sword from this stone is the rightful king of all England."

Gnngh!

Each of the noblemen tried to pull the sword from the stone. Not one of them could move it.

28

"It's impossible!" cried one.
"It's a trick," moaned another.
Merlin just smiled.

At that moment, a young
man rushed into the square. It
was Arthur.

"Is there a swordsmith nearby?" he asked. "I've come to buy a sword for my brother, Kay."

A big nobleman looked at the skinny boy. "Why not take the one in that stone?" he laughed.

"Yes," chuckled another. "It's yours if you can shift it."

"Thank you, sir," said Arthur.

He gripped the hilt of the mighty sword. With one smooth movement, he pulled it free.

A gasp came from the crowd. Then everyone knelt down and bowed their heads.

Long live the king!

Arthur was puzzled. "What's going on?" he asked.

Merlin emerged from the shadows. "I'll explain everything, your Majesty. Follow me."

And the wise wizard led Arthur back to the palace as king, just as he had planned.

Chapter 4

The enchanted trap

Some years later, King Arthur fell in love with the beautiful Lady Guinevere.

They held a huge wedding
at their castle in Camelot, and
invited hundreds of guests.

After the ceremony, there
was feasting, singing and
dancing in the great hall.

35

Arthur and his new bride
danced happily together.
Merlin looked on with pride.

One of the other dancers
caught his eye. She was a
stunning lady named Nimue.

Merlin fell hopelessly in love with her on the spot. After that, he visited Nimue every day.

He bought her gifts and told her how much he loved her. "I love you too," she said.

But Nimue was lying. She'd heard the stories about Merlin. "I could never love the son of a demon," she thought to herself.

"But if he thinks I love him, he'll teach me magic."

Merlin would do anything for Nimue. As time passed, he told her many of his secrets.

He taught her how to...

turn one object
into another...

fly through
the air...

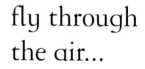

see through walls...

and even control the weather.

"You're as beautiful as a princess," he said one day. "You deserve a home to match."

He took Nimue to a vast
lake at the heart of a forest.
"This will be our home," he
cried, with a wave of his staff.

There was a thunderous roar and a swirl of stars. The next second, a towering palace appeared on the lake.

"Only we will know the palace is here," said Merlin. "It will be invisible to anyone else."

Nimue frowned.
"You and I shall live here forever," continued Merlin.

This was too much for
Nimue. "I could never spend
eternity with a demon's son,"
she snapped.

What?

With that, she reached out to
Merlin. Bolts of lightning flew
from her fingertips.

45

With a crash, glass rocks
burst out of the ground. They
rose around Merlin, trapping
him inside.

You taught me
too well, Merlin.

Merlin tried to fight the
magic. "Stop, I command you!"
he bellowed. But it was too late.

"You'll sleep forever in this invisible cave," called Nimue, as she floated away.

Merlin's love had led him into a trap. And now – who knows? Perhaps he's still there today.

The Legend of Merlin

Stories of Merlin have been told since the 6th century AD. They may have been based on the life of a Welsh prophet called Myrddin (c. 540-c.584). In the 12th century, a Welsh author named Geoffrey of Monmouth (c.1100-1155) wrote some stories which confused Myrddin with a warrior named Ambrosius Aurelianus, and called his character Merlin.

Arthurian consultant: John Matthews
Series editor: Lesley Sims

First published in 2012 by Usborne Publishing Ltd., Usborne House, 83-85 Saffron Hill, London EC1N 8RT, England. www.usborne.com
Copyright © 2012 Usborne Publishing Ltd.